MR. MEN
IN IRELAND

Roger Hargreaves

Original concept by
Roger Hargreaves

Written and illustrated by
Adam Hargreaves

EGMONT

Mr Quiet was enjoying a quiet walk when he met the one person he did not want to meet. Mr Chatterbox!

"Hello, hello, hello," chattered Mr Chatterbox. "You're very quiet aren't you, Mr Quiet? You need to get out more and chat. Like me! In fact, what you need is to learn the gift of the gab! Now, what is the gift of the gab I hear you say? It means that you can chat with ease. In fact, there's a stone in Ireland called the Blarney Stone and if you kiss it you will be granted the gift of the gab. We should go!"

And before Mr Quiet could say a word it had all been settled.

They were going to Ireland.

And, as it turned out, lots of their other friends wanted to join them. Especially, Little Miss Lucky.

She wanted to see the shamrock, the clover which is the symbol of Ireland, but most of all she wanted to find a four-leaf clover.

Little Miss Lucky had a lucky horseshoe and a lucky number seven, but the one thing she did not have was a four-leaf clover, which was even luckier because they were so difficult to find.

But being as lucky as Little Miss Lucky was, she found one as soon as they arrived!

Sightseeing around Ireland was going to be such fun.

As they set off everyone was in a very jolly mood.

Mr Chatterbox was chattily jolly.

Mr Noisy was noisily jolly.

Little Miss Splendid was splendidly jolly.

And Mr Quiet was quietly jolly.

There were so many ways to be jolly!

The first stop on their trip was the city of Belfast, where they visited Titanic Belfast.

The Titanic was one of the biggest passenger ships ever built, but it hit an iceberg on its maiden voyage. The Titanic Experience is an enormous exhibition which tells the story of the famous ship.

The front of the building looked like the prow of the Titanic and was just as big.

"You could never be described as titanic," said Mr Rude looking down at Mr Small.

"More like pint-sized, or puny, or titchy," he sniggered, rudely.

"And I could say the same of you," chuckled Mr Tall.

The next morning, they drove to Carrick-a-Rede, where they decided to walk across the famous cable bridge, suspended high above the sea.

However, as they crossed the bridge, it began to sink. Down it dropped, until they all had their feet in the sea! What had happened?

"Mr Greedy," asked Little Miss Splendid, "how many Ulster frys did you eat this morning?"

"One or two," replied Mr Greedy, sheepishly.

"And then two or three more!" replied Little Miss Splendid, crossly, looking at her very wet shoes!

Mr Greedy was so heavy that the cables had stretched under his weight and weighed the bridge down!

It wasn't long before Mr Greedy wanted to eat again. When they stopped for a picnic lunch at White Park Bay, there were cows on the beach!

Mr Silly thought this was wonderfully silly.

"Cows on a beach!" he exclaimed. "How silly! They'll be lying in deckchairs and making sandcastles before we know it!"

Can you imagine that?

Further along the coast they discovered the Giant's Causeway, where they climbed over the strange rock formations.

Mr Jelly was rather nervous.

"Do you think there are real giants?" he worried.

Suddenly an enormous voice boomed out.

"FEE FI FO FUM! I SMELL THE BLOOD OF A JELLY MAN!"

Mr Jelly shrieked and jumped in the air in fright.

But it was not a giant, it was Mr Noisy.

Mr Jelly was not amused.

They then took the ferry across to Rathlin Island to spend the night there.

But Mr Chatterbox was so busy chatting that he drove off the ferry before it had arrived.

SPLASH!

Now, Little Miss Splendid had a wet hat as well as wet shoes!

But at least she met some of the local wildlife!

They all dried off overnight, but when Mr Quiet saw their Galway fishing boat the next day, he didn't believe they'd be dry for long.

Especially with Mr Bump on board!

But amazingly, they did all manage to stay dry.

And they even caught some fish.

I'm sure you didn't expect that!

Maybe, Little Miss Lucky's four-leaf clover had something to do with that!

After their fishing trip they sailed on further to the Aran Islands, which are famous for their woolly fishermen's jumpers.

Even Mr Greedy found one to fit him, although it seemed to be shrinking!

Naughty, Little Miss Naughty!

Mr Chatterbox was full of facts about Ireland, very long-winded facts.

He told them that it was also known as the Emerald Isle because the grass is so lush and green, which meant the cows produced the best milk to make the most delicious butter.

But there was something else it was perfect for.

It was perfect camouflage for Mr Nosey.

All the better for being nosy!

They drove across the lush Irish countryside to Dublin.
A beautiful university city set on the banks of the
River Liffey.

That evening they went to a pub for supper.
Mr Chatterbox was in his element, for it was here that
he discovered the true Irish gift for the gab!

He spent the whole night chatting like he had never
chatted before. But when he caught up with the others
the next day, something had happened.

Something terrible.

He had lost his voice!

Oddly, his friends did not seem as concerned. In fact,
they seemed strangely happier!

So it was a much happier and quieter journey to the town of Kilkenny.

But things didn't remain quiet for long.

There was an arts festival on, with theatre and singing and dancing.

Mr Noisy couldn't help himself and joined in the folk singing.

He sang all night long.

And he lost his voice as well!

So, it was an even quieter journey to their final destination the next day.

Blarney Castle.

And the famous Blarney Stone.

Mr Quiet was not at all sure that he wanted the gift of the gab. He was really very happy living the quiet life, but he did not want to disappoint Mr Chatterbox.

So, Mr Strong hung him by his feet in front of the stone, which was the only way to reach it, and he kissed the stone.

Everyone held their breath in anticipation.

Had it worked? Had Mr Quiet got the gift of the gab?

And then he began to chatter and chatter and chatter. But the funny thing was they could barely hear him. The stone had made him chattier, but it had not made him louder!

And because Mr Chatterbox and Mr Noisy had lost their voices, their trip to Ireland ended on a much quieter note than anyone could have expected.

Mr Quiet was very happy.

"Well," said Little Miss Lucky to Mr Quiet, "you know what they call that?"

"What?" smiled Mr Quiet.

"The luck of the Irish!"

And she gave Mr Quiet the second four-leaf clover she had found.